This book belongs to:

_____

_____

_____

First published 1999 by Walker Books Ltd
87 Vauxhall Walk, London SE11 5HJ

This edition published 2011

2 4 6 8 10 9 7 5 3 1

© 1999 Lucy Cousins
Lucy Cousins font © 1999 Lucy Cousins

"Maisy" Audio Visual Series produced by King Rollo Films for
Universal Pictures International Visual Programming

Maisy™. Maisy is a registered trademark of Walker Books Ltd, London.

Printed in China

British Library Cataloguing in Publication Data:
a catalogue record for this book is available from the British Library

ISBN 978-1-4063-3475-3

www.walker.co.uk
www.maisyfun.co.uk

Maisy Makes Gingerbread

Lucy Cousins

WALKER BOOKS
AND SUBSIDIARIES

LONDON • BOSTON • SYDNEY • AUCKLAND

Maisy is in her kitchen today.

She is going to make gingerbread.

Maisy needs flour, sugar, butter, eggs and ginger.

Maisy mixes
everything
together.

She rolls out the mixture and cuts different shapes.

Maisy puts the gingerbread into the oven.

Maisy licks the bowl while the gingerbread is cooking.

Then she washes up.
Ding-dong!
That's the doorbell!
Who can it be?

It's Charley and Tallulah!

Just in time for afternoon tea.

Yum, yum!
Nice gingerbread,
Maisy.

Read and enjoy the Maisy story books

Maisy Dresses Up

A Maisy Story Book Lucy Cousins

Maisy's Bedtime

A Maisy Story Book Lucy Cousins

Maisy's Pool

A Maisy Story Book Lucy Cousins

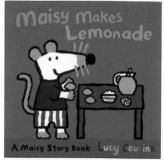

Maisy Makes Lemonade

A Maisy Story Book Lucy Cousins

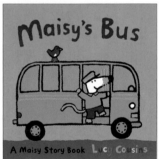

Maisy's Bus

A Maisy Story Book Lucy Cousins

Maisy Tidies Up

A Maisy Story Book Lucy Cousins

Maisy Makes Gingerbread

A Maisy Story Book Lucy Cousins

Maisy's Bathtime

A Maisy Story Book Lucy Cousins

My friend Maisy

Doctor Maisy

A Maisy Story Book Lucy Cousins

Maisy Goes Shopping

A Maisy Story Book Lucy Cousins

Available from all good booksellers

It's more fun with Maisy!